Lin Yi's Lantern
A Moon Festival Tale

Written by
Brenda Williams

Illustrated by
Benjamin Lacombe

'Now, tell me again what you are to buy from the market,' said Lin Yi's mother.

Lin Yi counted the items off on his fingers as he repeated the list once more. 'Moon cakes, star fruit, rice, yams . . . and peanuts for Uncle Hui.'

'Good boy,' said his mother.

'Can I buy a red rabbit lantern for the Moon Festival — please?' begged Lin Yi.

'Well, that is up to you,' said his mother. 'I have no more money to spare, but if you bargain well at the market you may have enough left for a red rabbit lantern.'

Lin Yi smiled happily. 'That won't be a problem, I can bargain better than anyone I know.'

He turned to go, reciting the list like a poem as he walked away.

'Moon cakes, star fruit, rice, yams . . .'

'. . . and don't forget the peanuts for Uncle Hui. You know how much he likes them,' his mother called after him.

As Lin Yi cycled to market, he smiled and
waved to people working in the rice paddies.

Very soon he saw Uncle Hui checking the fish
drying outside his house.

'Are you well, Uncle Hui?' asked Lin Yi.

'Yes, thank you,' Uncle Hui answered as he turned
the last fish towards the sun.

'I'm off to the market,' said Lin Yi. 'If I bargain well,
Mother says I can buy a red rabbit lantern with the change.'

'And will you be taking it to the picnic tonight?' asked
Uncle Hui.

'Yes. Will you be climbing the mountain with us, Uncle Hui?'

'Of course!' said Uncle Hui. 'I may be getting old, but I still enjoy
moon cakes and peanuts. Good luck with your bargaining.'

Lin Yi grinned happily and hurried on his way.

Lin Yi smiled as he passed under the moon gate. 'That will bring me luck in my bargaining at the market,' he thought. 'And I shall now live for five minutes longer.'

In the market, Lin Yi stopped to look longingly at the toffee apples.

'Do you want to buy one?' asked the trader.

'No, thank you,' said Lin Yi. 'I have to buy moon cakes, star fruit, rice, yams and . . . and I mustn't forget the peanuts for Uncle Hui. But if I bargain well, mother says I may buy a red rabbit lantern with the change.'

'But my toffee apples are very good,' said the trader. 'You could buy one of these and still have money to spare.'

'They look delicious,' said Lin Yi, 'but I really want a red rabbit lantern for the festival tonight.'

'Goodbye then,' said the trader, smiling. 'Maybe you will change your mind later on.'

Lin Yi knew he wouldn't change his mind. He really, really wanted a red rabbit lantern, even more than a toffee apple.

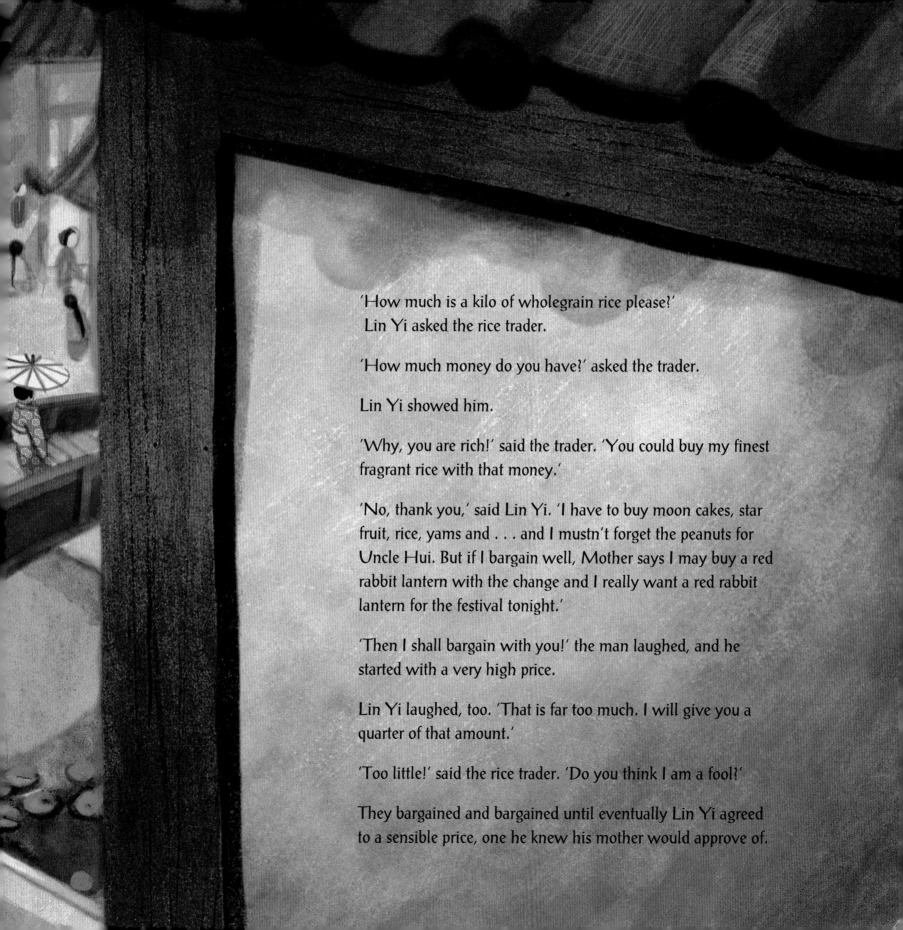

'How much is a kilo of wholegrain rice please?'
Lin Yi asked the rice trader.

'How much money do you have?' asked the trader.

Lin Yi showed him.

'Why, you are rich!' said the trader. 'You could buy my finest
fragrant rice with that money.'

'No, thank you,' said Lin Yi. 'I have to buy moon cakes, star
fruit, rice, yams and . . . and I mustn't forget the peanuts for
Uncle Hui. But if I bargain well, Mother says I may buy a red
rabbit lantern with the change and I really want a red rabbit
lantern for the festival tonight.'

'Then I shall bargain with you!' the man laughed, and he
started with a very high price.

Lin Yi laughed, too. 'That is far too much. I will give you a
quarter of that amount.'

'Too little!' said the rice trader. 'Do you think I am a fool?'

They bargained and bargained until eventually Lin Yi agreed
to a sensible price, one he knew his mother would approve of.

Lin Yi was feeling very pleased with himself after buying
the rice for such a good price. He was beginning to enjoy his
shopping. So when he bought the star fruit, he bargained hard,
and once more he did very well.

At the next stand, he paused to look at a little dough figure.
He wanted to buy one to play with. But then he reminded
himself that he would need to keep all the money he could if
he wanted to get a red rabbit lantern, so he moved on to buy
some yams.

Again he bargained well and put the yams into his basket
with the star fruit and the rice.

'Now,' Lin Yi thought, 'I have only the moon cakes and the
peanuts for Uncle Hui to buy.'

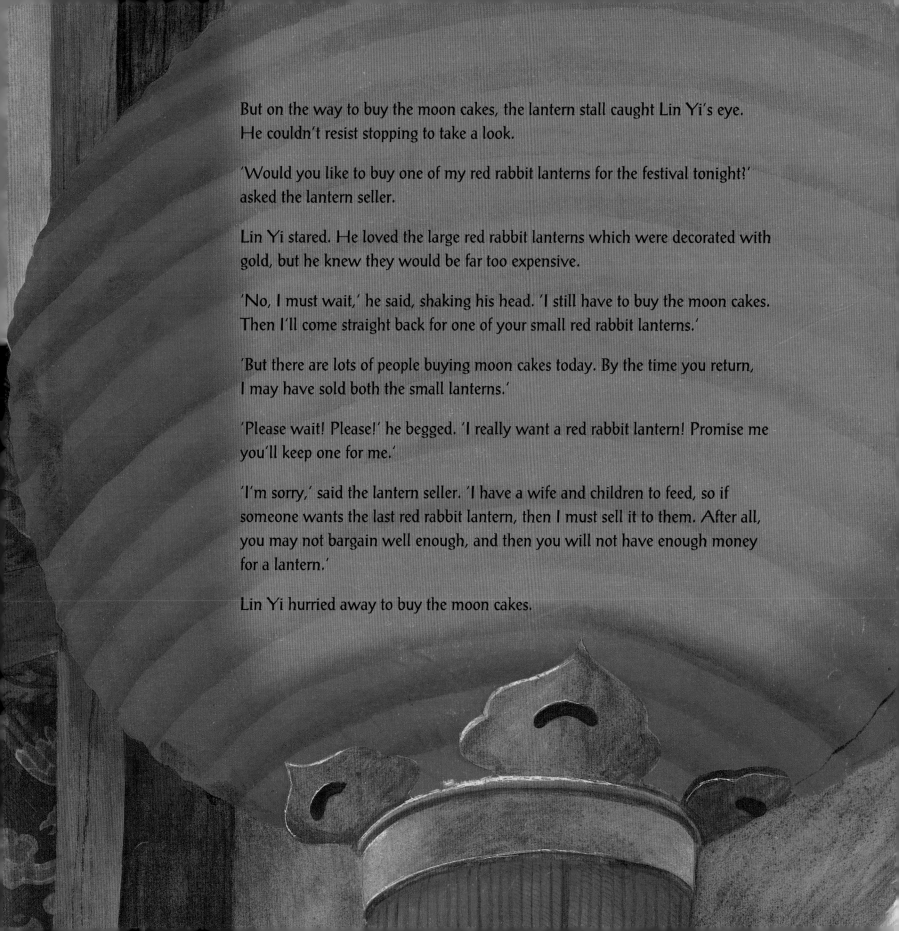

But on the way to buy the moon cakes, the lantern stall caught Lin Yi's eye. He couldn't resist stopping to take a look.

'Would you like to buy one of my red rabbit lanterns for the festival tonight?' asked the lantern seller.

Lin Yi stared. He loved the large red rabbit lanterns which were decorated with gold, but he knew they would be far too expensive.

'No, I must wait,' he said, shaking his head. 'I still have to buy the moon cakes. Then I'll come straight back for one of your small red rabbit lanterns.'

'But there are lots of people buying moon cakes today. By the time you return, I may have sold both the small lanterns.'

'Please wait! Please!' he begged. 'I really want a red rabbit lantern! Promise me you'll keep one for me.'

'I'm sorry,' said the lantern seller. 'I have a wife and children to feed, so if someone wants the last red rabbit lantern, then I must sell it to them. After all, you may not bargain well enough, and then you will not have enough money for a lantern.'

Lin Yi hurried away to buy the moon cakes.

'At last,' he thought, arranging the moon cakes in his basket. 'Now I am ready to buy the red rabbit lantern.'

Just then a woman walked past, munching peanuts, and he suddenly remembered Uncle Hui.

'Oh no,' he thought, 'I forgot to buy the peanuts!'

He counted his money carefully. Even if he bargained well, he knew he would not have enough to buy peanuts and a lantern. His heart sank right down to his sandals. He had tried so hard, and now it seemed that his dream was over.

He stood still for a while, trying to decide what to do. He so wanted the lantern, but he also knew how much Uncle Hui loved peanuts.

Biting his lip and wiping away his tears, Lin Yi turned firmly away from the lanterns and went to buy Uncle Hui's peanuts.

Sadly, Lin Yi pedalled home without
his red rabbit lantern.

'You are a good boy, Lin Yi,' said his mother. 'You have bought everything we need for our picnic. We have beautiful moon cakes, decorated with the Jade Hare and the Moon Fairy. We have the star fruit, and they will be delicious. You must have bargained well – especially for the rice and yams. But Lin Yi, what about your red rabbit lantern? Didn't you manage to buy even a small one!'

'No,' said Lin Yi bravely, trying not to cry. 'But there will be others I can see at the festival tonight. It doesn't matter.'

But of course, in his heart it did matter. It mattered very much.

Still, Lin Yi tried not to show it. Instead, he took the peanuts and gave them to Uncle Hui with a big smile.

'Thank you, Lin Yi,' said Uncle Hui. 'Now, I have a present for you.'

Lin Yi was speechless as he saw the red rabbit lantern.

'Oh, thank you! Thank you, Uncle Hui!' he exclaimed. 'It is beautiful! Far better than any lantern I dreamed of having!' And he beamed with happiness. 'How did you know that I didn't have enough money left to buy one?' he asked.

'Well,' said Uncle Hui with a twinkle in his eye, 'let's just say that during the Moon Festival time, many special things can happen, especially if you pass through the moon gate. We don't ask the reason, we are just happy.'

And side by side they climbed the moonlit mountain, Uncle Hui munching his peanuts as Lin Yi proudly carried his glowing red rabbit lantern.

THE LEGEND OF THE MOON FAIRY
AS TOLD BY UNCLE HUI

Long, long ago, when China was at the very centre of the world, the Earth had not one, but ten suns circling around it. Each of these suns would take turns shining on the Earth, which was a very beautiful place, with its sparkling rivers that kept the land fresh and watered for the crops to grow.

One day, mysteriously, all the suns began to shine on the Earth together. The people became very hot, the rivers started to dry up, and the land was cracked and parched. The emperor begged for someone to save the Earth before all the animals died from thirst, the soil became dust and there was nothing left for people to eat or drink.

For a long time, no one knew what to do. But then one of the emperor's finest archers, a man called Hou Yi, offered to shoot down all but one of the suns. The emperor was delighted to think that at last someone had come up with a clever and practical way to save the Earth.

Hou Yi took careful aim and one by one he shot down nine suns. People were calling Hou Yi a hero, so to thank him the emperor gave him a reward of a magic potion. It was made from a secret recipe of herbs, which would let him live forever.

That night, Hou Yi left the potion beside him and fell into a deep sleep. His wife, Chang-O, wanted to be immortal, so she took the potion and quickly drank it down. Finding herself floating upwards, Chang-O danced her way to the moon. When the people on Earth saw Chang-O, they began to call her the Moon Fairy.

Chang-O was very happy living on the moon. She built herself a crystal moon palace, and made friends with a kind and gentle hare. He explained that he had once offered himself as food to three wise fairies, who were disguised as hungry old men. As a reward for his amazing offer they allowed him to come and live on the moon. He became known as the Jade Hare.

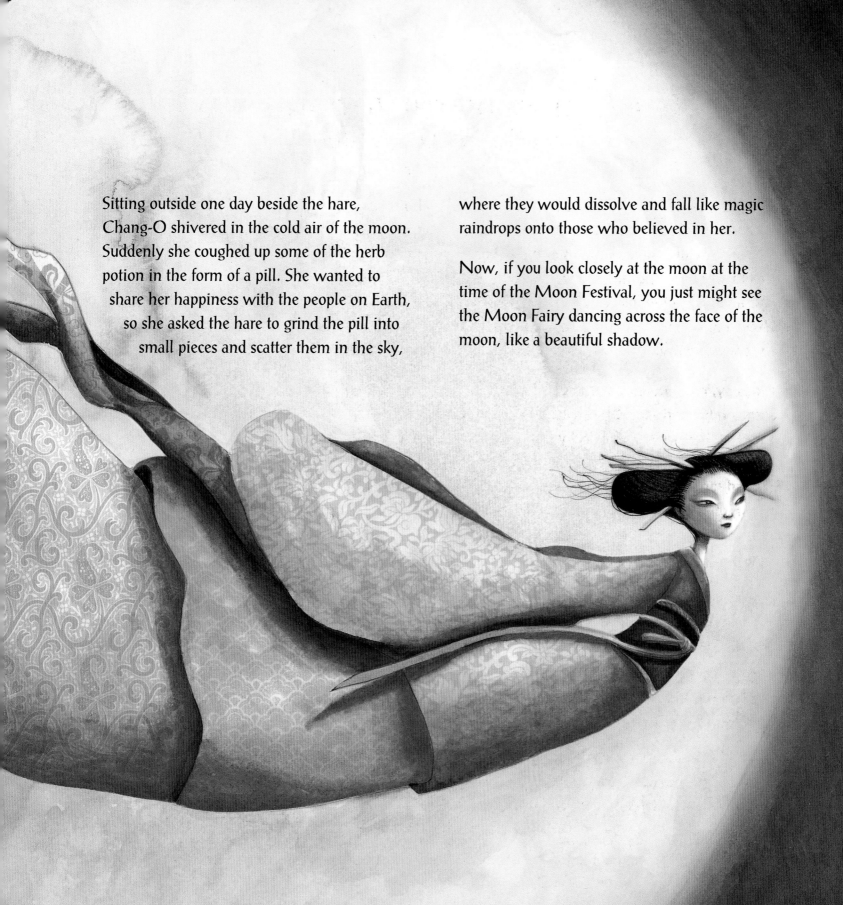

Sitting outside one day beside the hare, Chang-O shivered in the cold air of the moon. Suddenly she coughed up some of the herb potion in the form of a pill. She wanted to share her happiness with the people on Earth, so she asked the hare to grind the pill into small pieces and scatter them in the sky, where they would dissolve and fall like magic raindrops onto those who believed in her.

Now, if you look closely at the moon at the time of the Moon Festival, you just might see the Moon Fairy dancing across the face of the moon, like a beautiful shadow.

MAKE A CHINESE LANTERN

Chinese lanterns are made from paper and bamboo formed into shapes such as rabbits, butterflies or lobsters. You can create your own paper lantern by following these steps:

1. Decorate a piece of A4 paper.

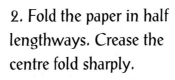

2. Fold the paper in half lengthways. Crease the centre fold sharply.

3. Hold the paper with the fold at the bottom, and start cutting towards the opposite open edge, approximately 3cm in from the narrow side. Do not cut all the way up; leave approximately 3cm of uncut paper at the top.

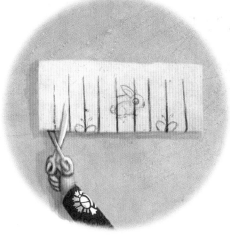

4. Repeat step 3, cutting eight more slits at 3cm intervals along the centre fold.

5. Open up the paper.

6. Apply glue to one short end and roll and attach it to the other to form a 'tube'. Gently push the top down slightly to form the lantern shape.

7. Cut a narrow strip of paper and glue it to the top of the lantern to make a handle.

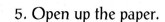

MARKET LIFE IN CHINA

Markets in small, rural towns in China are usually found in the town centre along a wide, main street. They are lined on either side by shops that display their goods out in the open. The markets are filled with many different sounds, smells and wonderful colours.

Fruit and vegetables are piled high on tables and can include watermelons, ginger, garlic, bamboo shoots, bean sprouts, pak choi — a kind of cabbage — squashes, yams, sweet potatoes, eggplants, very large white radishes and long beans.

The Chinese abacus is often used by traders to add up a customer's bill, as they find it faster than a modern calculator when working with large numbers. They shake the abacus to attract attention from potential shoppers.

Small groups of men sit together to play dice. The men bet by placing money between three dice; if they win, they are given a slice of duck. If not, they lose their money. Acrobats can sometimes be seen performing with gongs; there may also be balancing acts.

Market traders walk around wearing traditional yokes — or wooden bars — across their shoulders with a large basket suspended on each end. Depending on the wares, these might be flat or bowl shaped.

Chinese rural markets are busy, bustling places, crowded and noisy, with the sound of bicycle bells, birds singing, and stall holders shouting out their wares. Shoppers haggle with the traders, and chatter to their friends, passing on news and gossip. The market provides a wonderful meeting place, and offers a day out for the family.

Often people eat right in the market. There are round, wooden tables, sometimes with a hot pot in the centre. The pot can be for soup or oil. People sit on small, low stools around the tables.

There are always many people on bicycles in the market. It is estimated that over 300 million Chinese people ride a bicycle. Those leaving the market are often weighed down with live chickens or ducks hanging from racks on the back!

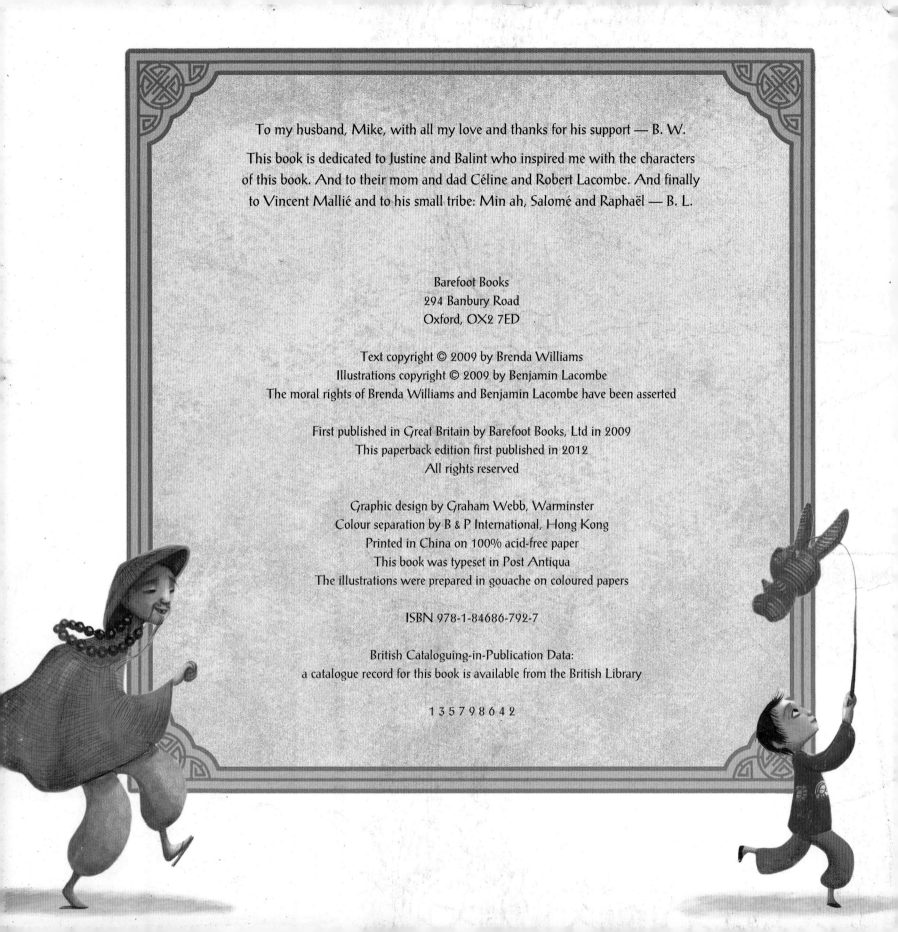

To my husband, Mike, with all my love and thanks for his support — B. W.

This book is dedicated to Justine and Balint who inspired me with the characters
of this book. And to their mom and dad Céline and Robert Lacombe. And finally
to Vincent Mallié and to his small tribe: Min ah, Salomé and Raphaël — B. L.

Barefoot Books
294 Banbury Road
Oxford, OX2 7ED

First published in Great Britain by Barefoot Books, Ltd in 2009
This paperback edition first published in 2012

Graphic design by Graham Webb, Warminster
Colour separation by B & P International, Hong Kong
Printed in China on 100% acid-free paper
This book was typeset in Post Antiqua
The illustrations were prepared in gouache on coloured papers

ISBN 978-1-84686-792-7

British Cataloguing-in-Publication Data:
a catalogue record for this book is available from the British Library

1 3 5 7 9 8 6 4 2